CONTINENTS OF THE WORLD

DISCOVERING ANTARCTICA'S
LAND, PEOPLE, AND WILDLIFE

A MyReportLinks.com Book

Amy Graham

 MyReportLinks.com Books

an imprint of

Enslow Publishers, Inc.

Box 398, 40 Industrial Road

Berkeley Heights, NJ 07922

USA

MyReportLinks.com Books, an imprint of Enslow Publishers, Inc. MyReportLinks®
is a registered trademark of Enslow Publishers, Inc.

Library of Congress Cataloging-in-Publication Data

Graham, Amy.
  Discovering Antarctica's land, people, and wildlife / Amy Graham.
    v. cm. — (Continents of the world)
Includes bibliographical references and index.
Contents: Antarctica: the base of the world — Land and climate — Plant
and animal life — People and their impact — Science and discovery —
History and exploration.
  ISBN 0-7660-5205-2
  1. Antarctica—Juvenile literature. 2. Natural
history—Antarctica—Juvenile literature. [1. Antarctica.] I. Title.
II. Series.
  G863.G73 2004
  919.8'9—dc22
                        2003014516

Printed in the United States of America

10 9 8 7 6 5 4 3 2 1

To Our Readers:
Through the purchase of this book, you and your library gain access to the Report Links that specifically back
up this book.
The Publisher will provide access to the Report Links that back up this book and will keep these Report Links
up to date on **www.myreportlinks.com** for three years from the book's first publication date.
We have done our best to make sure all Internet addresses in this book were active and appropriate when we
went to press. However, the author and the Publisher have no control over, and assume no liability for, the
material available on those Internet sites or on other Web sites they may link to.
The usage of the MyReportLinks.com Books Web site is subject to the terms and conditions stated on the
Usage Policy Statement on **www.myreportlinks.com**.
A password may be required to access the Report Links that back up this book. The password is found on the
bottom of page 4 of this book.
Any comments or suggestions can be sent by e-mail to comments@myreportlinks.com or to the address on
the back cover.

Photo Credits: Ardo X. Meyer, National Oceanic and Atmospheric Collection (NOAA) Corps
Collection, p. 3c; Artville, p. 1; Commander John Bortniak, NOAA/Department of Commerce,
pp. 36, 41, 44; © 1998–2003 The Antarctic Connection LLC, p. 28; © 2001–2003 Paul Ward,
pp. 17, 23; © Corel Corporation, pp. 3a, 3b, 10, 12, 15, 21,31; © 1998–2002. Centre for Atmospheric
Science, Cambridge University, UK., p. 33; Dan Shapiro, NOAA/Department of Commerce;
Dave Mobley, NOAA/Department of Commerce, p. 14; GeoAtlas, p. 9; Jonathan Shackleton, p. 43;
Michael Van Woert, NOAA/Department of Commerce, pp. 19, 29; MyReportLinks.com Book, p. 4;
NOAA/Department of Commerce, Sanctuary Collection, p. 40; Reproduced from the Dictionary of
American Portraits, published by Dover Publications, Inc., in 1967, p. 38; Scientific Committee on
Antarctic Research, p. 20; The National Science Foundation, p. 25; William Haxby/PBS, p. 34.

Cover Photo: Artville; Commander John Bortniak, National Oceanic and Atmospheric Collection
Corps Collection; © Corel Corporation.

Contents

MyReportLinks.com Books
Great Books, Great Links, Great for Research!

The Report Links listed on the following four pages can save you hours of research time by **instantly** bringing you to the best Web sites relating to your report topic.

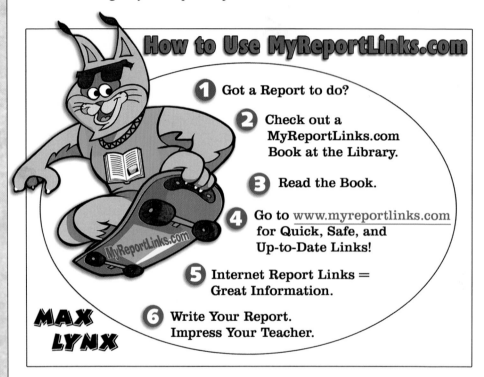

How to Use MyReportLinks.com

1 Got a Report to do?

2 Check out a MyReportLinks.com Book at the Library.

3 Read the Book.

4 Go to www.myreportlinks.com for Quick, Safe, and Up-to-Date Links!

5 Internet Report Links = Great Information.

6 Write Your Report. Impress Your Teacher.

MAX LYNX

The pre-evaluated Web sites are your links to source documents, photographs, illustrations, and maps. They also provide links to dozens—even hundreds—of Web sites about your report subject.

MyReportLinks.com Books and the MyReportLinks.com Web site save you time and make report writing easier than ever!

Report Links

 The Internet sites described below can be accessed at http://www.myreportlinks.com

▶**Secrets of the Ice**   *EDITOR'S CHOICE
This site follows a four-year Antarctic expedition and reports some of the latest global-change research findings. You can read about Antarctica's environment and the research being conducted there.

▶**The *World Factbook 2002*: Antarctica**   *EDITOR'S CHOICE
The site from the Central Intelligence Agency contains facts and figures about Antarctica. Here you can access data about Antarctic geography, people, government, economy, transportation, and communications as well as transnational issues.

▶**PBS *Nova*: Warnings from the Ice**   *EDITOR'S CHOICE
This PBS site is about climate change in Antarctica. Here you will find an interactive time line explaining the information encoded in the ice-core's frozen layers. The "Water World" section provides diagrams of what would happen if the West Antarctic Ice Sheet were to melt.

▶**GLACIER**   *EDITOR'S CHOICE
Rice University's GLACIER Web site is an introduction to Antarctica and the research performed there. Here you will find in-depth explorations of the science behind Antarctic weather, ice, and oceans.

▶**Cool Antarctica**   *EDITOR'S CHOICE
Cool Antarctica is a guide to the world's southernmost continent. Here you can learn about Antarctica's life, weather, biology, exploration, history, and much more.

▶**South Pole Observatory**   *EDITOR'S CHOICE
The South Pole Observatory is a United States scientific research facility located at the southernmost point on the globe. Here you will find information about South Pole science, life, and history. The site also features live cams, virtual tours of the facility, and dozens of images.

Report Links

The Internet sites described below can be accessed at
http://www.myreportlinks.com

▶**Antarctica: WBUR Journeys to Antarctica**

WBUR's Dan Grossman spent five weeks chronicling life in Antarctica. Here you can watch videos of penguins, take an interactive tour of Palmer Station, read Grossman's journal, and much more.

▶**Antarctic Connection**

Antarctic Connection is a travel, news, information, and retail site dedicated to the southernmost continent. Learn about Antarctic history, expeditions, wildlife, news, weather, and more.

▶**Antarctic Resources**

Gateway Antarctica is a center for Antarctic studies and research at the University of Canterbury in New Zealand. Their site contains aerial photographs, maps, documents, scientific articles, and more.

▶**Antarctic Sciences Section, Office of Polar Programs**

The United States Antarctic Program (USAP) is a government organization that supports research activities in Antarctica. Here you will learn facts about Antarctica and the research being performed there.

▶***The Antarctican***

The latest news and comments on life and research in Antarctica. The "Ice Picks" section contains the Antarctic photography of Doug Thost.

▶**Auroras: Paintings in the Sky**

The aurora australis is a visual phenomena only found in the Antarctic region. Here you will find a scientific explanation of auroras. This site also features images of this natural wonder from Earth and from space.

▶**British Antarctic Survey**

The British Antarctic Survey has performed studies in Antarctica for over fifty years. On their site you will learn about the continent of Antarctica and about the research they are conducting.

▶**The Committee for Environmental Protection**

The Protocol on Environmental Protection to the Antarctic Treaty was designed to protect Antarctica from environmentally damaging activities. You can learn about the agreement's background, member countries, and more.

Any comments? Contact us: **comments@myreportlinks.com**

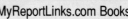
Report Links

▶**Diving Under Antarctic Ice**

A wide variety of animals inhabit the icy waters around Antarctica. This site contains photographs, journals, and other media from an underwater photography expedition.

▶**Exploring the Solar System with Meteorites from Antarctica**

More meteorites are collected in Antarctica than the rest of the world combined. This NASA site explains how meteorites found in Antarctica provide clues to the history of the universe.

▶**James Cook**

James Cook was the first explorer to cross the Antarctic Circle. Here you will find biographical information on this legendary navigator. Maps and accounts of Cook's three pioneering voyages are included.

▶**National Snow and Ice Data Center**

The National Snow and Ice Data Center supports polar and cryospheric research. This site contains in-depth information about glaciers, ice shelves, icebergs, freshwater ice, sea ice, permafrost, ice cores, and more.

▶**Antarctica: *Terra Australia Incognita***

Here you will find an in-depth look at Antarctica from *One World Magazine*. The site contains a wealth of information about explorers, the Antarctic Treaty, and the continent itself.

▶**Origins: Antarctic—Scientific Journeys from McMurdo to the Poles**

This Exploratorium site contains a wealth of information about the work being done at McMurdo Station in Antarctica. Here you will learn about penguins, different types of icebergs, Antarctic politics, and more.

▶**The Ozone Hole Tour**

This multimedia site from Cambridge University's Center for Atmospheric Science provides a comprehensive explanation of the ozone hole. Part II of the tour is dedicated exclusively to recent ozone loss over Antarctica.

▶**PBS American Experience: *Alone On the Ice***

Richard E. Byrd was the first person to fly over the South Pole. The official site of the PBS series *Alone on the Ice* is about Byrd and his adventures.

Report Links

▶**Seal Conservation Society: Pinniped Species Information Pages**

Antarctica has six species of seals. The Seals Conservation Society's site contains in-depth descriptions of these and other seals of the world. Information about species status and distribution can also be found here.

▶**Searchable Database of Antarctic Treaty Documents**

The Antarctic Treaty is an agreement between forty-five countries setting the boundaries for the uses of Antarctica. This site includes a searchable database of all of the documents of the treaty.

▶*70 South*: **The Number One Source for Antarcticles**

70 South is an interactive Web site containing news and information about Antarctica. Here you can learn about Antarctic history, explorers, wildlife, environment, bases, and more.

▶**Sir Ernest Henry Shackleton**

Sir Ernest Henry Shackleton led several pioneering Antarctic voyages. Here you will find information about his early life, expeditions, and more.

▶**South-Pole.com**

South-Pole.com is dedicated to the history of Antarctic exploration. In-depth information about explorers, expeditions, and more can be found here. You can also view time lines, maps, and images.

▶**Subglacial Antarctic Lake Exploration**

Thousands of meters below the surface lie the subglacial lakes of Antarctica. Here you will find research information, articles, images, and other resources related to these buried bodies of water.

▶**Welcome to the Ice**

Robert Holmes repairs automatic weather stations in Antarctica. On his site, you will find a time line of Antarctica's history, interesting facts, photographs, historic journals, and more.

▶**Welcome to the International Penguin Conservation Web Site**

Antarctica is home to five species of penguins. At the International Penguin Conservation Web site you will learn about these, as well as the other remaining species around the world. Learn about the threats to penguins and what is being done to protect them.

Land Area
5,100,021 square miles
(13,209,047 square
kilometers)

Highest Point of Elevation
Vinson Massif
16,066 feet (4,897 meters)

Lowest Point of Elevation
Bentley Subglacial Trench
8,327 feet below sea
level (−2,538 meters)

Major Mountain Ranges
- Antarctic Peninsula
- Ellsworth
- Prince Charles
- Transantarctic
- Whitmore

Major Glaciers
- Beardmore
- Lambert
- Rennick
- Support Force

Major Ice Shelves
- Amery
- Filcher
- Larsen
- Ronne
- Ross

Major United States Science Stations
- Amundsen-Scott South Pole Station
- McMurdo Station
- Palmer Station

All metric and Celsius measurements used in this text are approximate estimates.

Chapter 1

The Base of the World

The frozen continent of Antarctica covers about 5.1 million square miles (13.2 million km), or one tenth of all the world's land. It is the fifth largest of Earth's seven continents. The area is roughly one-and-a-half times the size of the United States. Despite its grand size, before 1820 no one had ever seen Antarctica. Since the times of the ancient Greeks, people speculated there might be land near the South Pole. The Greek philosopher Aristotle (384–322 B.C.) wrote about two cold regions at each of the poles. The word Antarctica comes from the Greek. *Ant* means

▲ There is almost no precipitation on Antarctica. Yet the continent contains 70 percent of Earth's freshwater.

opposite; *arktikos* refers to the bear constellation that marks the sky above the North Pole.[1] Mapmakers of the past even included the imagined land on their maps. They visualized a large southern continent they labeled *terra incognita*, or the unknown land.

Antarctica lay undiscovered for so long because few people dared to enter the dangerous seas around the continent. The winds and currents are ferocious, and the water is the coldest in the world. Floating icebergs fill the sea. Only a small portion of each iceberg is visible above the water. Some icebergs are the size of a ship; others are miles long. Before modern sailing equipment, sailing a ship through the icy Southern seas took more than talent. It also required great bravery. In 1773, the courageous world explorer Captain James Cook was the first person to cross the Antarctic Circle. He did not see Antarctica, but he did find several nearby islands. When he returned home to Britain, he brought back news of many seals and whales in these undisturbed waters.

The wildlife did not remain undisturbed for long. In the late 1700s, seal hunters from Britain and the United States arrived. Fur seals were highly prized for their pelts, which made warm, fashionable slippers. Sadly, greedy hunters slaughtered entire colonies of seals. They gave no thought to the future survival of the species. Fur seals came close to extinction within decades.[2] In 1820, the sealing boats pushed farther south in search of more fur pelts. In their travels, the sailors sighted land. They had stumbled across the fabled continent of Antarctica.

The land these sailors found was a cold, inhospitable place. Ice sheets and glaciers cover nearly 98 percent of Antarctica. Only the peaks of the tallest mountains are visible from beneath the blanket of ice. The ice is up to

two and three miles (3.2 and 4.8 km) thick. It is so heavy that the land buckles under its weight. The strain is great enough to submerge the land thousands of feet below sea level in places. Even so, the miles of towering ice make Antarctica the highest of the continents. The freezing, stormy Southern Ocean surrounds Antarctica on all sides. In some places along the shore, the sea itself is frozen all year long. This ice is called pack ice. Each winter, the pack ice extends farther out into the sea, gaining back the ice that had melted away in the summer. This almost doubles the size of the continent.

The Antarctic climate may not be well suited for people, but plenty of animals live along the shores and in the nearby ocean. Seals, penguins, whales, and fish that live

▲ *Weddell seal milk contains 60 percent fat. This causes cubs to rapidly gain blubber after birth. Blubber keeps them warm in the water and on the ice, where temperatures can drop to lower than −40°C.*

here have one thing in common: They are all specially adapted for living in the cold weather. The Weddell seal is a remarkable mammal that lives under ice all winter long. With their sharp teeth, the seals chew holes in the pack ice where they surface to breathe. Penguins are well protected from the cold by their thick, waterproof coat of feathers. Gentoo penguins have over seventy feathers per square inch.[3] When the temperatures rise above freezing, penguins can even overheat.

Since 1959, Antarctica has been set aside by the nations of the world for scientific study. No nation owns this continent. An international agreement called the Antarctic Treaty preserves this land as a world park dedicated to the study of science. The treaty also protects Antarctica's unique environment and wildlife. Countries have built more than forty science stations on Antarctica and nearby islands. Most scientists come to study for the summer season, while others spend the winter. Some even spend a year or two on the continent.

The United States operates three main science stations, including one at the South Pole. Some stations are equipped with comforts such as electricity, phones, and Internet access. Through human innovation, Antarctica is no longer as dangerous a place to visit as it once was. Still, the climate remains too hostile for people to stay for long. In the first place, it is simply too cold. In July 1983, a Russian station in East Antarctica recorded the coldest temperature on Earth. The temperature was an unbelievable −128°F (−89°C). Another challenge is the dark winters. During the winter months, the earth's rotation moves the Southern Hemisphere away from the sun. At the South Pole, the sun does not rise over the horizon for

From May until September, Antarctica remains dark. This is quite different from the summer months of November through February when the sun shines every day for twenty hours.

the entire winter. The land remains cast into darkness twenty-four-hours-a-day for months.

The seasons of the Southern Hemisphere are opposite those in the north. The long Antarctic winter starts in May and lasts into September. The short summer season is November through February. January is the warmest month. Coastal temperatures on the Antarctic peninsula average between 23°F (–5°C) and 40°F (4°C). Meanwhile, at the South Pole the temperature still remains well below 0°F (–18°C).[4] The summer sun is visible in the sky for up to twenty hours a day.

Sometimes Antarctica looks more like it could be on another planet. Along the coasts, huge cliffs of ice tower above the ocean. Where the ice sheets meet the sea, icebergs break off and float out into the ocean. On the interior of the continent, ice stretches in every direction. There are few signs of human presence in this remote and pristine land. Antarctica is home to some of the last wild places on Earth that remain untouched by humans.

Chapter 2

Land and Climate

Three oceans converge around Antarctica: the Atlantic, Indian, and Pacific. Where they meet, they are often called by one name: the Southern Ocean. Westerly winds form a strong ocean current that surrounds Antarctica. The Antarctic Circumpolar Current acts as a barrier, keeping out the warmer water of the oceans to the north. As the Antarctic ice sheets slowly melt, they add cold water to the Southern Ocean. This cold water sinks to the bottom of the ocean floor and moves north, cooling the world's oceans. In this way, Antarctica's ice cap plays a big role in the overall global climate.[1]

▲ Although they appear to be stationary, icebergs are slowly moving with the currents of the sea. Over time, wind erodes away some of the ice. This particular iceberg has a pointy shape, making it irregular.

▶ Ice Formation

The glaciers of Antarctica took millions of years to form. Years of snowfall slowly built up into dense layers of ice. As the weight of the ice increased, air pockets in the ice grew smaller and smaller. Eventually, the air pockets disappeared altogether and the ice was an impenetrable glacier.[2] Glaciers may look permanent and unmoving, but they are actually slowly creeping. The force of gravity and the pressure of their own massive weight cause them to inch along. They slowly flow from the center of the continent toward the coasts.

Ice follows a similar pattern to that of streams that flow into oceans. Glaciers flow into ice sheets. The edges of these ice sheets are also called ice shelves. Where the ice shelves meet the ocean, the ice rises and falls with the tide. Pieces of ice break away from the ice shelf, forming icebergs that float off to sea. This process of iceberg formation is called "calving."

There are three basic types of icebergs: tabular, irregular, and rounded. Newly calved icebergs are tabular, or shaped like a table. They have flat tops and sharply angled sides. As the iceberg moves into warmer water, it slowly dissolves and becomes irregular. The wind and saltwater wear down the ice and change its shape. The oldest icebergs are rounded. Rounded icebergs have lost most of their original mass.

The ocean around Antarctica is sometimes so cold that the saltwater freezes. When the water reaches 28.8°F (–2°C), ice crystals called *grease ice* form on the surface of the water. As the sea grows colder, the grease ice grows into a slushy *frazil ice*. The frazil ice thickens and forms circles of ice called *pancake ice*. The final stage of ice

🔺 *Shown here is sea ice in its earliest stages of formation.*

formation is thick *pack ice.* Parts of the sea near the coast are frozen into pack ice all year long.

▶ Climate

Winter temperatures in Antarctica routinely drop below –100°F (–73°C). The continent's high elevation is one reason for the cold. Even in the summer, when the sun is high in the sky most of the day, Antarctic temperatures rarely rise above 5°F (–15°C) in the interior of the continent. The coast is warmer, with a high of 40°F (4°C).[3] The permanent ice cover reflects most sunlight back into the atmosphere without soaking up its warmth. Antarctic winds can rage up to 200 miles per hour (321.9 km per

hour). Gravity pulls these strong gusts, called *katabatic* winds, down off the polar icecap.

It may be hard to believe, but Antarctica is one of the driest desert climates on Earth. The air is so cold that moisture freezes long before it reaches the ground. There has been no measurable precipitation near the South Pole for millions of years. During the frequent blizzards, most of the snow does not fall from the clouds. It is blown up from the ground by the ferocious winds.

Natural Phenomena

An aurora is a breathtaking sight in the skies near the North and South Poles. Pulsating, colored lights fill the dark sky with shades of purple, red, and green. This phenomena is called the aurora australis, or the southern lights. The aurora occurs when winds from the sun bring particles that get caught in the earth's magnetic field. The solar winds excite particles in the air. The particles then emit energy in the form of photons, or light.

Geography

The continent is divided into two major areas: East and West Antarctica. In the West is the Antarctic Peninsula, which reaches northward toward the tip of South America. The peninsula has a warmer climate than the rest of the continent. To the east of the peninsula is the Weddell Sea, which is frozen with thick pack ice even in the summer months most years. Antarctica's tallest mountain, Vinson Massif, is in the Sentinel Range of West Antarctica. The peak towers 16,062 feet (4,896m) above sea level. To the south is the Ross Sea region. This is where many of the historic explorers began their Antarctic adventures. A huge barrier of ice, called the Ross Ice Shelf,

▲ *The Ross Ice Shelf is the southernmost point on Earth that can be reached by boat.*

covers an area the size of France. The United States maintains its largest Antarctic science outpost, McMurdo Station, on Ross Island. The island is also home to Mount Erebus, a live volcano that belches out steam and smoke.

East Antarctica is a much larger region than its western counterpart. The Transantarctic Mountains separate the East from West. East Antarctica is an enormous plateau covered in ice. The South Pole is located on the high interior of this plateau. A ceremonial red-and-white striped pole marks the spot. Nearby, the United States maintains the Amundsen-Scott Science Station.

To the south of the Transantarctic Mountains are the amazing Dry Valleys of Victoria Land. These desert valleys at one time held glaciers but are now completely free of ice and snow. No rain has fallen there for over 2 million years.

East Antarctica is also home to many freshwater lakes located deep under the ice. The warmth of the earth's core slowly melts the bottom layers of the glacial ice. The melt-water pools in basins and forms lakes. The largest known of these freshwater lakes is Lake Vostok, located near the Russian Vostok science station. The water in these lakes may hold clues about the earth's climate millions of years ago when the water first froze. It is also possible that some life exists in these waters, completely isolated from the rest of the world. Scientists are eager to test the water, but it will take time to develop a way to sample the lakes without contaminating them.[4]

Vostok Station, located on Antarctica's East Sheet, was built in 1957 by Russia. The coldest temperature on Earth, −128.6°F (−89.2°C), was recorded here on July 21, 1983.

Chapter 3

Plant and Animal Life

For an ice-covered continent, Antarctica supports an amazing amount of life. There are not any grasses, trees, or shrubs there. Yet tiny plants are among the most plentiful life forms. The majority of plants in Antarctica are lichens, mosses, and algae. The Dry Valleys of Victoria Land are an unlikely place for plants. The land there is bare of snow and exposed to extreme cold and high winds. Amazingly, lichens make their home under the ground. They live in the sandstone, just under the surface of the rock. The sandstone provides a protected environment where they can grow. These lichens grow very slowly because little water and sunlight reach them each year. Some are thought to be over two hundred thousand years old.[1] Only two flowering plants are able to live on the continent. These are Antarctic hair grass (*Deschampsia antarctica*) and Antarctic pearlwort (*Colobanthus quitensis*), both of which live only on the Antarctic Peninsula.

Visitors to Antarctica can expect to see several species of penguin, including Adélie, (shown here) Chinstrap, Emperor, and Gentoo.

No land mammals, reptiles, or amphibians live on Antarctica. The largest insect on Antarctica is a wingless fly, or midge (*Belgica antarctica*), less than half an inch long (1.3 cm). Other Antarctic insects include spiders, fleas, and mites. Though not many animals or birds live on land, the seas around Antarctica are full of life. Seals, whales, fish, penguins, and other seabirds are plentiful.

▶ Penguins: At Home in the Cold

Seven species of penguins live in Antarctica or on the nearby islands. Only four types of penguins stay in Antarctica all year long. These are the emperor (*Aptenodytes forsteri*), Adélie (*Pygoscelis adeliae*), Chinstrap (*Pygoscelis antarctica*), and Southern Gentoo (*Pygoscelis papua elsworthii*) penguins.[2] Penguins cannot fly. Their short, stubby wings, or flippers, help them to swim and dive. Their flippers also come in handy while traveling over the ice. When they need to get somewhere in a hurry, penguins flop onto their bellies and use their wings to push themselves along. This is called tobogganing.

Penguins' feathers are extremely thick. The birds spend hours each day preening, or maintaining their feathers. While preening, they cover their feathers with oil from a gland near their tail. The oil keeps the water from reaching their skin. The thick layer of blubber underneath their coat of feathers helps to keep them warm.

Penguins are seabirds, and they spend most of their time at sea and on the ice. When it is time to raise their young, they come ashore to rocky nesting places called rookeries. The mother and father penguins work together to build a rounded nest from pebbles. There is not much space, so the nests are built very close together. Once the mother lays one or two eggs, the parents take turns sitting on the nest to keep the eggs warm. When the chick hatches, the parents take turns going out to sea to find food. The hungry chick sticks its mouth into his parent's bill to feed on regurgitated food. As the chicks get older, they require more food. Both parents leave to hunt, while the chicks huddle together in a large group called a *crèche*. As a group the chicks are less likely to be preyed upon by hungry birds called South Polar skuas.

Dedicated Dads

The large emperor penguin is the biggest of all the penguins. They average three-and-a-half feet (1.1 m) tall. Unlike other penguins, the emperor penguins hatch their

▲ Snow petrels live along the coasts of Antarctica, including the Antarctic Peninsula, because their diet consists mainly of krill. Unlike most Antarctic species, snow petrels do not live in colonies.

babies in the dead of the Antarctic winter. The female lays an egg, which the male puts in a pouch near his feet. The mother then returns to the sea to feed, while the father stays behind with the egg. For sixty-four long days, the males huddle together in the frigid winter cold. They never leave their eggs, even to eat. By the time the chicks hatch, the fathers have lost almost half their body weight. The mothers then return to feed the chick.

Penguins may be the most well-known Antarctic birds, but many other seabirds live in the region, too. Petrels, gulls, skuas, sheathbills, terns, cormorants, and albatross are common sights. The albatross, with its huge wingspan of up to eight feet, likes to follow the wake of ships in the Southern Ocean. Sailors consider the friendly albatross a good omen.

▷ Seals of the Antarctic

Six species of seals live in Antarctica. These are the Ross, Weddell, Antarctic fur, crabeater, leopard, and southern elephant seals. The Weddell seal is the only one to spend all year there. Despite its name, the crabeater seal does not eat crabs. Its diet is almost exclusively made up of a shrimp-like animal called *krill*. The Ross seal is a bit of a mystery. Since they live out on the thick pack ice where few people have ever gone, little is known about them. Sealers once hunted the Antarctic fur seal close to extinction. Luckily, the seals have been able to make a full recovery, thanks to restrictions put in place in the 1970s. Southern elephant seals were also the target of hunters, who used their blubber for oil. These enormous creatures are the largest of the seals. Southern elephant males can weigh almost 4 tons (4.1 metric tons) and reach 15 feet

(4.6 m) in length. They are able to dive underwater for up to two hours without coming up for a breath of air.[3]

Ocean Life

The fish that live in the icy waters of the Southern Ocean must contend with freezing temperatures. Some of the fish have chemicals, called glycopeptides, flowing through their blood. The glycopeptides act as antifreeze. They allow these fish to inhabit waters where other fish would freeze to death. One unusual Antarctic fish is the white-blooded ice fish of the species *Channichthyidae.* It is the only animal with a vertebra, or backbone, that does not

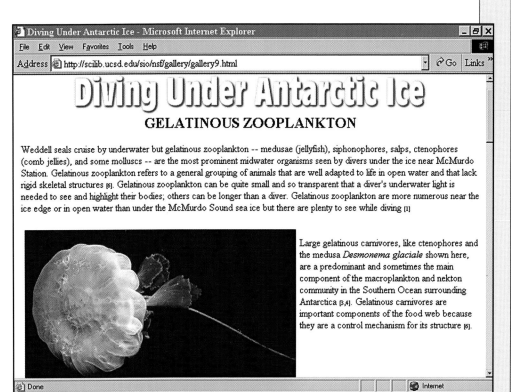

Diving Under Antarctic Ice - Microsoft Internet Explorer

File   Edit   View   Favorites   Tools   Help

Address http://scilib.ucsd.edu/sio/nsf/gallery/gallery9.html   Go   Links

Diving Under Antarctic Ice
GELATINOUS ZOOPLANKTON

Weddell seals cruise by underwater but gelatinous zooplankton -- medusae (jellyfish), siphonophores, salps, ctenophores (comb jellies), and some molluscs -- are the most prominent midwater organisms seen by divers under the ice near McMurdo Station. Gelatinous zooplankton refers to a general grouping of animals that are well adapted to life in open water and that lack rigid skeletal structures [6]. Gelatinous zooplankton can be quite small and so transparent that a diver's underwater light is needed to see and highlight their bodies; others can be longer than a diver. Gelatinous zooplankton are more numerous near the ice edge or in open water than under the McMurdo Sound sea ice but there are plenty to see while diving [1]

Large gelatinous carnivores, like ctenophores and the medusa *Desmonema glaciale* shown here, are a predominant and sometimes the main component of the macroplankton and nekton community in the Southern Ocean surrounding Antarctica [3,4]. Gelatinous carnivores are important components of the food web because they are a control mechanism for its structure [6].

Done   Internet

The medusa Desmonema glaciale *shown here is a kind of zooplankton found most commonly in the open water and ice edges of the Southern Ocean.*

have red blood cells. Ice fish have developed other ways of moving oxygen that require less energy. By conserving their energy, they are able to thrive in the cold polar water.

Krill

Antarctic krill (*Euphasia superba*) is a tiny, shrimp-like organism that lives in the Southern Ocean. This crustacean forms the basis of the Antarctic food chain. It feeds on algae and other phytoplankton. Many animals eat krill—from fish and seabirds, to seals, penguins, and baleen whales. Baleen whales have plates on either side of their mouths. These baleen plates act like a filter, allowing food in and keeping excess water out. Each summer, baleen whales migrate to the Southern Ocean to feed on the krill swarms. They return to warmer oceans to mate and raise their young. Baleen whales include blue, sei, fin, minke, humpback, and right whales. Two toothed whales live in the Southern Ocean as well: orcas (also called killer whales) and sperm whales. Sperm whales eat squid. Orcas eat fish, penguins, seals and even other whales.

Chapter 4 ▶

People and Their Impact

Early explorers of Antarctica battled against the elements just to stay alive. They rarely considered the impact of their actions on the Antarctic environment. The hunters who slaughtered seals and whales to the point of extinction did not think of the long-term health of the Antarctic ecosystem. The future of the Antarctic continent depends on people and how we choose to treat it.

▶ Life at a Science Station

Twenty-seven nations send scientists to work in Antarctica. The United States operates the largest of the science stations, McMurdo Station on Ross Island. This outpost was first established in 1956. Today, McMurdo looks more like a small mining town than a science outpost. It has a hospital, church, restaurants, gym, and a post office, as well as laboratories. Up to 1,200 people spend the Antarctic summer at McMurdo, while a crew of just 250 stays through the long winter.[1] The United States military maintains the country's Antarctic science stations. The scientists who work there are not government officials. They come mostly from American colleges and universities.

Governments first built science bases with convenience in mind. Trash was considered too expensive to remove. Workers hauled garbage out onto the ice where it would sink into the ocean when the ice thawed. At McMurdo Station, the United States burned trash in an open pit with no regard to controlling the emissions.[2]

First established in 1956 and composed of over one hundred structures, McMurdo Station is the largest settlement in Antarctica. Approximately 1,200 people take up residence here in the summer, while only about 250 stay during the winter.

Fortunately, in 1990, the United States began a recycling program at McMurdo. Now all of the station's waste, excluding human waste, is removed from Antarctica.

Tourism

In the late twentieth century, people started to travel to Antarctica for a new reason: sightseeing. The Antarctic appeals to adventurous tourists. Rugged outdoor enthusiasts come to experience mountain climbing, scuba diving, sea kayaking, or camping. Most tourists are there to view the scenic icebergs, amazing cliffs of ice, and plentiful wildlife. Penguins and seals are easy to spot. They come ashore to raise their young during the summer months when Antarctica is approachable by ship. Some tourists get to visit the remains of the early adventurers' huts. These shacks, now one hundred years old or more, are preserved by the frigid cold weather. Visiting the huts is regulated. Still, about one thousand people get to enter them each year.

Most tourists arrive on icebreaker "cruise ships." Icebreakers are ships designed to cut a path through the frozen ocean. These ships have a round bottom that allows them to float on top of the ice. Then the weight of the heavy ship breaks the pack ice. The round bottom means an icebreaker rocks in the water more than a regular boat, up to a 45 degree angle.[3] The icebreakers pick up passengers from port cities in Argentina, Chile, South Africa, Australia, and New Zealand. With their passengers on

▲ Even during the summer months, the average temperature of Antarctica is below 0°F (–18°C). For cruise ships to travel through Antarctic waters, they must be able to break through the pack ice.

board, they then make the trek through the cold waters to Antarctica. The ships make stops along the Antarctic coast so travelers may go ashore to sightsee. For these excursions the crews use small, black, rubber boats with outboard motors called zodiacs.

During the 2000–01 summer season, 12,248 tourists visited Antarctica.[4] There are two ways to look at the growing Antarctic travel industry. The more people who visit the continent, the more spoiled Antarctica becomes. After all, part of the beauty of Antarctica is its remoteness from the populated world. More people mean more pollution and more wear and tear on the landscape. More people could mean more competition with the native wildlife for the few spots sheltered from the extreme weather. Plants grow so slowly in the cold that just one footstep on a patch of lichens can cause severe damage.

Yet tourism may not be a bad thing. The waste surrounding the science stations horrified the first tourists. They brought the issue to international attention and demanded the science stations clean up their acts. Travelers come to Antarctica to view a pristine landscape that they can find nowhere else in the world. Tourists may be a strong voice for the health of the southern continent. Many return and explain to others how important it is that the continent be protected.[5]

Mining in Antarctica

Presently, Antarctica is governed by the Antarctic Treaty, which has forty-five member countries. The treaty states that Antarctica may only be used for peaceful, scientific purposes. It bans military activity and nuclear waste dumping. The original Antarctic Treaty did not touch upon the subject of natural resources.

Mining through the deep ice cover would be very expensive. Still this remains an important issue. In the not-so-distant future, people may deplete other sources of fossil fuels. If that happens, Antarctic mining might look more attractive.

Environmentalists worry that mining would have dramatic effects on the delicate Antarctic ecosystem. In 1991, the Antarctic Treaty member nations signed an agreement called the Protocol on Environmental Protection. The protocol, which came into effect in 1998, bans mining in the Antarctic for fifty years. It also establishes environmental guidelines for all of the governments who do research in Antarctica.

▲ *Antarctica's pristine landscape has rarely been disturbed.*

Chapter 5

Science and Discovery

The Antarctic Treaty system defines the Antarctic as a peaceful place dedicated to scientific study. Where else on Earth does science come first? Antarctica is an extraordinary place for the study of science. As there is no native human population, the continent is largely unspoiled. The animals remain friendly and curious, unafraid of humans. The freezing cold weather allows fewer species to survive there. As a result, scientists have fewer factors to take into account when studying the ecosystem.

Astronomers need clear, dark skies to peer out into the universe. Antarctica's high altitude and long, dark, winter nights make it a great place to view the stars. Although pollution does reach the Antarctic environment, compared to other areas of the world, it is remarkably free of air and light pollution. The dry climate is another benefit because there is little water in the air to block the view of outer space.

▷ Ozone Hole: Sunscreen Needed

Scientists on the frozen continent are also working to understand the hole in the ozone layer. Ozone is a naturally occurring gas in the earth's atmosphere. Ozone plays an important role—it filters out harmful ultraviolet rays from the sun. Ultraviolet rays can cause skin cancer and other health problems. Too much exposure to ultraviolet rays has harmful effects on the earth's climate and ecosystems as well. In 1985, British scientists studying at Halley

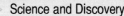

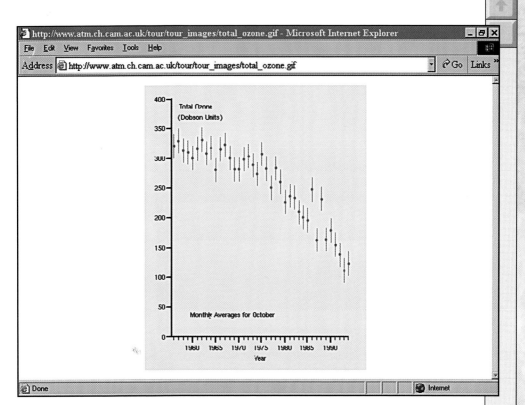

http://www.atm.ch.cam.ac.uk/tour/tour_images/total_ozone.gif - Microsoft Internet Explorer

File   Edit   View   Favorites   Tools   Help

Address   http://www.atm.ch.cam.ac.uk/tour/tour_images/total_ozone.gif   Go   Links

Total Ozone
(Dobson Units)

Monthly Averages for October

Year

Done   Internet

▲ This graph shows the decrease in total ozone over the Halley Bay Research Station in Antarctica. The presence of CFCs in the earth's atmosphere caused the amount of ozone to drop by more than 50 percent between the early 1970s and mid-1990s.

Bay Research Station, near the Weddell Sea, first discovered a hole in the ozone layer above Antarctica. The hole in the ozone layer focused the world's attention on the problem of ozone depletion. Today, visitors to Antarctica must be cautious and wear plenty of sunscreen to avoid severe sunburn.

Scientists now widely recognize that the thinning of the ozone layer is due to human activity. Chemicals such as chlorofluorocarbons, or CFCs, rise into the atmosphere, where they break down and destroy the ozone layer. People used CFCs in refrigerators, industrial solvents, and

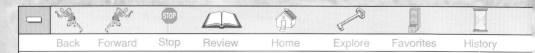
spray cans. In 1995, production of these substances ended in the United States and much of the world. According to the United States Department of Environmental Protection, the ozone layer could recover within fifty years if steps are taken worldwide to stop production of these harmful chemicals.[1]

▶ A Warmer Planet

Global warming is another topic of research in Antarctica. The temperature of the earth's atmosphere is rising. If it continues to rise at the same rate, the earth's climate will change. Experts believe that an excess of greenhouse gases

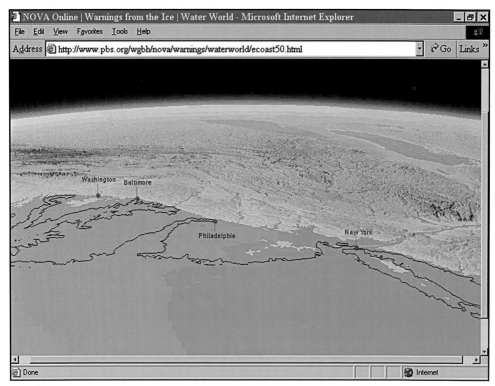

NOVA Online | Warnings from the Ice | Water World - Microsoft Internet Explorer

File   Edit   View   Favorites   Tools   Help

Address http://www.pbs.org/wgbh/nova/warnings/waterworld/ecoast50.html   Go   Links

Washington   Baltimore

Philadelphia   New York

Done   Internet

▲ *If the East Sheet of Antarctica melted, the waters off the east coast of the United States are expected to rise 170 feet. The cities of Philadelphia, New York, Washington, D.C., and Baltimore would be submerged in water.*

is to blame. Greenhouse gases in the earth's atmosphere keep the sun's heat from escaping back into space. Carbon dioxide is one example of a greenhouse gas. This gas is produced when we burn fossil fuels, such as coal, oil, and natural gas. Carbon dioxide is to blame for about half of the problem of global warming.[2]

Scientists who study climate change are interested in the polar ice caps. One concern is that global warming will increase the rate at which the polar ice caps melt. Much of the planet's freshwater is stored in this glacial ice. If it melted, the level of water in the ocean would rise, flooding coastlines and changing the world's climate. Current studies of the ice cap report mixed findings. Some parts of Antarctica, such as the Antarctic Peninsula, do seem to have warmed up quickly within the last fifty years. Some other studies show that the polar ice cap is actually growing thicker. It is difficult for scientists to understand climate change based on a few years of data because climate change occurs slowly over thousands of years.[3]

Rocks from Space

The Antarctic ice holds clues to the beginnings of the solar system in the form of meteorites. Meteorites are ancient rocks that have fallen to Earth from space. Most come from asteroids or comets, but some originate from the moon or other planets. Meteorites land all over the earth, but Antarctica has a wealth of them. The cold preserves the rocks. They fall on the surface of the ice and become buried in the glacier over the course of time. The glacier flows toward the sea, carrying the meteorites with it. Sometimes the creeping glacier hits an obstacle, like the Transantarctic Mountains, on its way to the ocean. Then the ice is slowly worn away by the wind, exposing the

▲ *The Ceremonial South Pole, located at the South Pole, is surrounded by the flags of those countries that signed the Antarctic Treaty, an international agreement to protect Antarctica's environment.*

meteorites. The dark rocks are easy to spot against the white ice cap.

The United States and Japan are the only two countries presently collecting meteorites in Antarctica. The United States collects several hundred meteorites from there each year. The samples are frozen and sent to the Johnson Space Center in Houston, Texas, where they are preserved and studied. In the laboratory, scientists can determine when the meteorite fell to Earth and where it is likely to have come from. One ancient Mars meteorite is thought to contain fossils of bacteria, which would prove Mars once supported life.[4]

Fossils: A Key to the Past

Antarctica is also a plentiful source for fossils, another key to the past. Fossils are records of plant and animal life suspended in ancient rock. Plant fossils and petrified wood found there show that Antarctica once supported plant life. Fragments of land mammals and reptiles indicate that the climate used to be much warmer. Some of the more interesting fossil finds include a now-extinct giant penguin that towered over six feet (1.8 m) tall and an ancient sea turtle as big as a car.[5]

Fossils helped scientists to discover that the earth's continents were once connected. Fossil records show that the same species of land animals once lived on continents now separated by the world's oceans. It is impossible that these land animals could have crossed these waters. So how did they come to be on different continents? The explanation is that, at one time, the continents were all together. Antarctica was once part of a large supercontinent. Over millions of years, the continents shifted and broke apart.

Chapter 6

History and Exploration

Captain Cook came close to discovering Antarctica in the early 1770s, when he crossed the Antarctic Circle. After Cook's voyage, Antarctica remained unknown for another fifty years. Then, in 1820, Russian naval commander Fabian von Bellingshausen entered the Southern Ocean. On January 27, 1820, he spotted Antarctica. He is considered by many to be the first person to see the continent. Several months later, American and British sealers spotted the Antarctic Peninsula while searching out more seal colonies.

▶ **Early Exploration**

In the late 1830s, several countries sent explorers to learn more about the southern continent. James Clark Ross led a British excursion from 1839 to 1843. Sailing in his two ships, the *Erebus* and the *Terror*, Ross and his men discovered the Ross Ice Shelf,

◀ *Ship Commander James Cook, later to become Captain Cook, circled Antarctica in 1772. He was unable to see the land due to the ice that surrounded it.*

a huge wall of ice stretching along the coast for hundreds of miles. In places, the ice towered 180 feet (54.9 m) above the water. In 1840, French explorer Jules-Sébastien-César Dumont d'Urville discovered a land near the South Pole he called *Terre Adèlie*, after his wife. American Charles Wilkes charted over 1,200 miles (1,931 km) of the East Antarctic coastline. Despite their discoveries, the world lost interest in Antarctica for the next fifty years. It remained largely ignored until the late 1890s when interest in whaling brought people back to the Southern Ocean.

▷ Whaling Days

In 1904, the first whaling station was built in the Antarctic at a location called South Georgia Island. Whale blubber was used to produce oil, an important source of fuel before the widespread use of electricity. Hunters killed the whales with harpoons, and then dragged the huge carcasses back to the whaling station. At the station, workers removed the whale blubber. By the 1930s, whalers slaughtered as many as forty thousand whales each year. At that rate, the whales were quickly headed for extinction. Most targeted were right, humpback, blue, fin, and sperm whales. Today an international whaling commission protects these species.

The blue whale (*Balaenoptera musculus*) is one of the largest animals to ever have lived. A grown adult is over eighty feet (24.4 m) long and weighs over one hundred tons (101.6 metric tons). Sadly, scientists believe the blue whale population is less than 3 percent of its original numbers, thanks to overhunting by humans.[1] Biologists now understand that the Southern Ocean is an important feeding ground for whales. Commercial whaling is illegal in the

▲ *Although blue whales can be found in every ocean, they feed in waters in or near the polar regions, especially during the summer. Krill are plentiful at this time of year, and blue whales have been found with as much as one ton of food in their stomach during this feeding season.*

Southern Ocean, which was declared a whale refuge in 1994.[2]

Race for the Pole

Today most people reach the South Pole by airplane. When the first people journeyed to the South Pole, they had to trek across hundreds of miles of snow on cross-country skis. When they arrived, there was no science station where they could warm up and resupply. In every direction, all they could see was a flat land of ice and snow.

It was not until the early 1900s that explorers set out to reach the South Pole. Several times, teams of courageous men tried and failed. The conditions were difficult, even deadly. The men faced physical hardships such as frostbite and scurvy. We now know scurvy is caused by a diet without enough vitamin C, but then no one understood the disease. The human body can only store six weeks worth of vitamin C. Without fresh food to supply the vitamin, scurvy set in. Scurvy causes teeth and gum rot, stomach pain, fatigue, bleeding, and eventually death.[3]

In the winter of 1911–12, two national teams competed to see who could first reach the longitude of 90 degrees South. Explorer Roald Amundsen led a team from Norway. He and his men used sled dogs and cross-country skis to traverse the ice. On December 14, 1911, the Norwegian party arrived at their destination. They raised a tent and flew their country's flag at the southern-most point on Earth, the South Pole.

British explorer Robert Falcon Scott led the second team involved in the race for the pole. His party of five

This hut, located at Cape Evans, was built by members of Robert Falcon Scott's crew in January 1911. It was restored as close to its original condition as possible in 1960. It was from this shelter that Scott and his men left on their trip to the South Pole.

men hauled their own sleds instead of using dogs. Just thirty-five days after Amundsen, Scott reached the Pole. In the most heartbreaking Antarctic tragedy, Scott and his party never made it back. Blizzard conditions kept the exhausted, disheartened men from reaching their food stashes in time. All five of the men died of starvation and exhaustion. Despite their tragic end, their voyage played an important role in understanding Antarctica. When a search party discovered their bodies the next spring, they also found fossil specimens the party had collected. These fossils helped scientists to understand that long ago, Antarctica had been a warmer place where plants and land animals lived.[4]

Shackleton's *Endurance*

Sir Ernest Shackleton set off on one of the most famous Antarctic voyages in 1914. His dream was to become the first person to cross the entire continent, but it was not to be. His crew never even set foot on Antarctica. Their ship, the *Endurance*, became trapped in pack ice in the Weddell Sea at the beginning of the expedition. Slowly the pack ice crushed the *Endurance*, and the men were forced to abandon ship.

Camping on the ice, they made their way across the frozen sea to small, uninhabited Elephant Island. There most of the men spent a freezing winter in a shelter made of snow and two wooden boats lashed together. Shackleton and five men set off in the third boat in a desperate attempt to go for help. The men faced stormy seas and incredible odds. The boat made it over eight hundred miles in sixteen days to South Georgia Island. Shackleton then crossed an ice-covered mountain range to reach the whaling station on the other side of the island. He

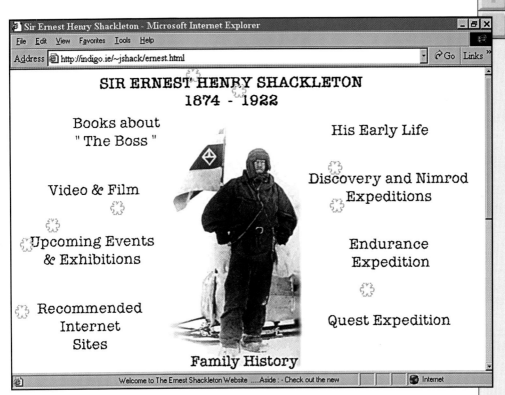

Sir Ernest Henry Shackleton - Microsoft Internet Explorer

File   Edit   View   Favorites   Tools   Help

Address http://indigo.ie/~jshack/ernest.html   Go   Links »

SIR ERNEST HENRY SHACKLETON
1874 - 1922

Books about
" The Boss "

His Early Life

Video & Film

Discovery and Nimrod
Expeditions

Upcoming Events
& Exhibitions

Endurance
Expedition

Recommended
Internet
Sites

Quest Expedition

Family History

Welcome to The Ernest Shackleton Website .....Aside : - Check out the new   Internet

▲ *Sir Ernest Shackleton's 1914 attempt to cross the Antarctic continent ended in failure when his boat, the* Endurance, *became trapped in ice on the Weddell Sea for eleven months.*

returned as soon as the ice allowed the next spring to fetch the rest of his crew. Miraculously every single one of the men returned home alive.

▶ Exploration in the Age of Technology

Airplanes made it easier to explore the frozen continent. In November 1929, American Richard Evelyn Byrd became the first person to fly over the South Pole. He greatly increased the United States' knowledge of the Antarctic landscape through his aerial photography and map-making efforts. Seven countries—Argentina,

▲ *The international community continues to make efforts to preserve the beauty of Antarctica.*

Australia, Chile, France, New Zealand, Norway, and the United Kingdom—officially claimed parts of Antarctica as their own. After World War II, many countries built outposts on the ice. They served to provide shelter for scientists and also to stake a claim. The United States and USSR did not claim Antarctic land, although they both reserved the right to do so.[5]

The span from 1957 to 1958 was an important time in Antarctic history. Over sixty of the world's countries participated in a project called the International Geophysical Year (IGY). Countries with claims agreed to set aside their conflicts and cooperate in the name of science. Twelve countries built stations on Antarctica during the IGY. The effort was a huge success. The coordination among the countries convinced their leaders to sign the Antarctic Treaty, which continues the spirit of peaceful, scientific cooperation in Antarctica to this day.

Chapter Notes

Chapter 1. The Base of the World

1. Walker Chapman, *The Loneliest Continent* (Greenwich, Conn.: New York Graphic Society Publishers, Ltd., 1964), p. 2.

2. John May, *The Greenpeace Book of Antarctica* (New York: Doubleday, 1989), p. 142.

3. Bruce McMillan, *Penguins at Home: Gentoos of Antarctica* (Boston: Houghton Mifflin Company, 1993), p. 15.

4. Jeff Rubin, *Lonely Planet: Antarctica,* 2nd ed. (Oakland, Calif.: Lonely Planet Publications, 2000), p. 54.

Chapter 2. Land and Climate

1. Jeff Rubin, *Lonely Planet: Antarctica,* 2nd ed. (Oakland, Calif.: Lonely Planet Publications, 2000), p. 176.

2. John May, *The Greenpeace Book of Antarctica* (New York: Doubleday, 1989), p. 24.

3. Antarctic Connection, "Antarctic Weather," n.d., <http://www.antarcticconnection.com/antarctic/weather/index.shtml> (January 12, 2003).

4. Scientific Committee on Antarctic Research, "Subglacial Antarctic Lake Exploration," n.d., <http://salegos-scar.montana.edu/> (January 19, 2003).

Chapter 3. Plant and Animal Life

1. Jeff Rubin, *Lonely Planet: Antarctica*, 2nd ed. (Oakland, Calif.: Lonely Planet Publications, 2000), p. 183.

2. Bruce McMillan, *Penguins at Home: Gentoos of the Antarctica* (Boston: Houghton Mifflin Company, 1993), p. 30.

3. Antarctic Connection, "Wildlife of Antarctica," n.d., <http://www.antarcticconnection.com/antarctic/wildlife/seals/s_elephant.shtml> (January 12, 2003).

Chapter 4. People and Their Impact

1. National Science Foundation Office of Polar Programs, "Your Stay at McMurdo Station Antarctica: McMurdo Station," n.d., <http://www.theice.org/mcmstay.html#history> (January 26, 2003).

2. John May, *The Greenpeace Book of Antarctica* (New York: Doubleday, 1989), p. 134.

3. Woods Hole Oceanographic Institute, "WHOI At Sea-Online Expeditions," n. d., <http://www.whoi.edu/home/marine/expeditions_buesseler_letter1a.html> (January 26, 2003).

4. The CIA World Factbook, "Overview of the Antarctic Economy," n.d., <http://www.odci.gov/cia/publications/factbook/geos/ay.html#People> (January 26, 2003).

5. Christopher Joyner, Professor of Government and Foreign Service, Georgetown University, in critique of manuscript, July 18, 2003.

Chapter 5. Science and Discovery

1. U.S. Environmental Protection Agency, "Ozone Depletion," n.d., <http://www.epa.gov/ozone/science/q_a.html#q3> (January 19, 2003).

2. U.S. Department of Energy's Atmospheric Radiation Measurement Program Education Site, "Causes of Global Warming," n.d., <http://www.arm.gov/docs/education/globwarm/causglobwarm .html> (January 19, 2003).

3. "Antarctica Gives Mixed Signals on Warming," *National Geographic,* n.d., <http://news.nationalgeographic.com/news/2002/ 01/0125_020125_antarcticaclimate.htm> (January 19, 2003).

4. Johnson Space Center-NASA, "Life on Mars?" n.d., <http:// www-curator.jsc.nasa.gov/curator/antmet/marsmets/life.htm> (January 20, 2003).

5. Jeff Rubin, *Lonely Planet: Antarctica,* 2nd ed. (Oakland, Calif.: Lonely Planet Publications, 2000), p. 304.

Chapter 6. History and Exploration

1. American Cetacean Society, "Blue Whale Fact Sheet," n.d., <http://www.acsonline.org/factpack/bluewhl.htm> (January 25, 2003).

2. International Whaling Commission, "Whale Sanctuaries," n.d., <http://www.iwcoffice.org/Catches.htm#Sanctuaries> (January 20, 2003).

3. Tony Horwitz, *Blue Latitudes* (New York: Henry Holt and Co., 2002), pp. 33–34.

4. Edwin Mickleburgh, *Beyond the Frozen Sea: Visions of Antarctica* (New York: St. Martin's Press, 1987), p. 95.

5. United States Central Intelligence Agency, *The World Factbook: Antarctica,* n.d., <http://www.odci.gov/cia/publications/factbook/geos/ ay.html#People> (January 25, 2003).

Further Reading

Armstrong, Jennifer. *Shipwreck at the Bottom of the World: The Extraordinary True Story of Shackleton and the Endurance.* New York: Crown, 1998.

Baines, John D. *Antarctica.* Austin, Tex.: Raintree Steck-Vaughn Publishers, 1997.

Bramwell, Marytn. *Australia, the Pacific, and Antarctica.* Minneapolis, Minn.: Lerner Publications, 2001.

Gaines, Ann Graham. *Captain Cook Explores the Pacific in World History.* Berkeley Heights, N.J.: Enslow Publishers, Inc., 2002.

George, Michael. *Antarctica: Land of Endless Water.* Mankato, Minn.: The Creative Company, 2002.

Hooper, Meredith. *Antarctic Journal.* Washington, D.C.: National Geographic Society, 2000.

Langley, Andrew. *The Great Polar Adventure: The Journey of Roald Amundsen.* Broomall, Pa.: Chelsea House Publishers, 1995.

Riddle, John. *Robert F. Scott.* Broomall, Pa.: Mason Crest Publishers, 2002.

Sayre, April Pulley. *Antarctica.* Brookfield, Conn.: Twenty-First Century Books, Incorporated, 1998.

Swan, Robert. *Destination: Antarctica.* New York: Scholastic, Incorporated, 1999.

Wheeler, Sara. *Greetings from Antarctica.* Columbus, Ohio: McGraw-Hill Children's Publishing, 1999.

Woods, Michael. *Science on Ice: Research in the Antarctic.* Brookfield, Conn.: Millbrook Press, 1995.